398.2   Bierhorst, John.
B   Doctor Coyote

PERMA-BOUND®

DATE DUE			

$11.45

DOCTOR COYOTE

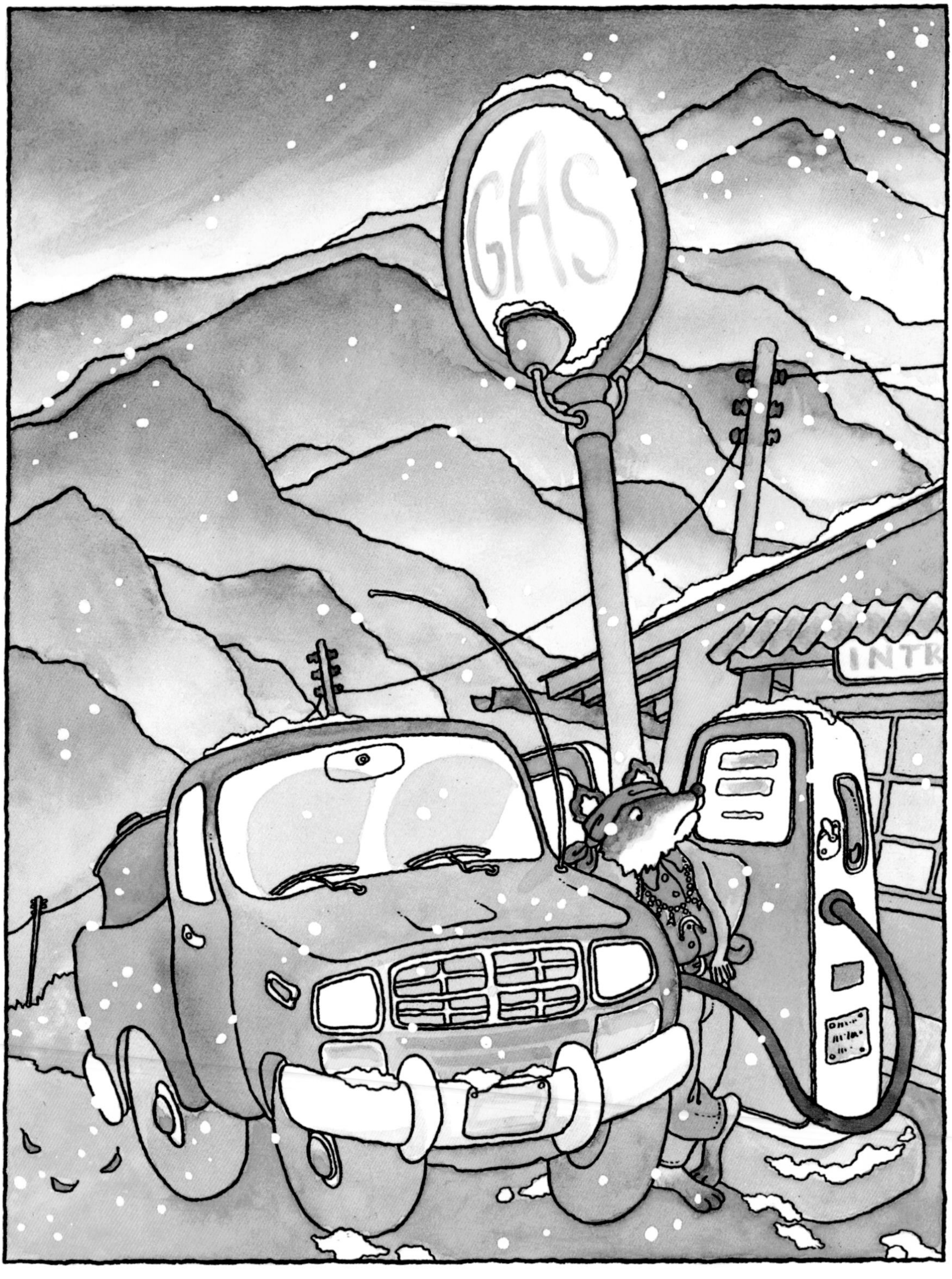
GAS
INTR

DOCTOR COYOTE

A Native American Aesop's Fables

RETOLD BY JOHN BIERHORST

PICTURES BY WENDY WATSON

Aladdin Paperbacks

First Aladdin Paperbacks edition August 1996
Text copyright © 1987 by John Bierhorst
Illustrations copyright © 1987 by Wendy Watson

Aladdin Paperbacks
An imprint of Simon & Schuster
Children's Publishing Division
1230 Avenue of the Americas
New York, NY 10020

Also available in a Simon & Schuster Books for Young Readers edition
Designed by Jane Byers Bierhorst
The text of this book was set in ITC Galliard.
The illustrations were done in pen-and-ink with watercolor.
Printed and bound in China

10   9   8   7   6   5   4   3   2   1

The Library of Congress has cataloged the hardcover edition as follows:
Bierhorst, John.
Doctor Coyote: a native American Aesop's fables.
Summary: Coyote is featured in each of these Aztec fables.
1. Aztecs—Legends.   2. Indians of Mexico—Legends.   3. Coyote (Legendary character)
4. Fables.   [1. Aztecs—Legends.   2. Indians of Mexico—Legends.
3. Coyote (Legendary character)   4. Fables]   I. Watson, Wendy, ill.   II. Title.
F1219.76.F65B55   1987   398.2'452974442   86-8669
ISBN 0-02-709780-3
ISBN 0-689-80739-2 (Aladdin pbk.)

Less than a hundred years after Columbus discovered the New World, a ship from Spain crossed the Atlantic carrying a book of Aesop's fables. These were the famous animal stories that had been told in Europe since Greek and Roman times. Once in America they fell into the hands of Aztec Indians, who saw them as trickster tales and in retelling them made the Native American Coyote the chief character. Old as they are, the fables that follow, retold from the Aztec, are among Coyote's newer adventures. At the same time they take us back to a storytelling tradition that is even older than Greece and Rome.

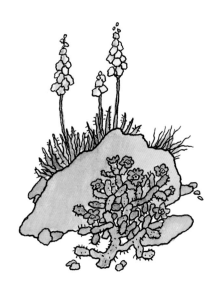

*Here begin stories and sayings made up by a
wise man named Aesop, in which he
shows us how to live carefully.*

Coyote used to stay at home. I don't know why, but he would never go anywhere. When he got hungry, he would eat the turkeys he had on hand. Pretty soon his turkeys were all gone.

Then he started to eat his sheep, and pretty soon his sheep were all gone too.

Then he started to eat the horses that pulled his plow. And when his horses were almost eaten up, his dogs got together and had a meeting, and this is what they said.

"Friends, come gather around. If Coyote eats the horses that pull his plow, what will he do to us? Let's not waste time. Let's go." And with that they all ran away. *Give a rampage plenty of room.*

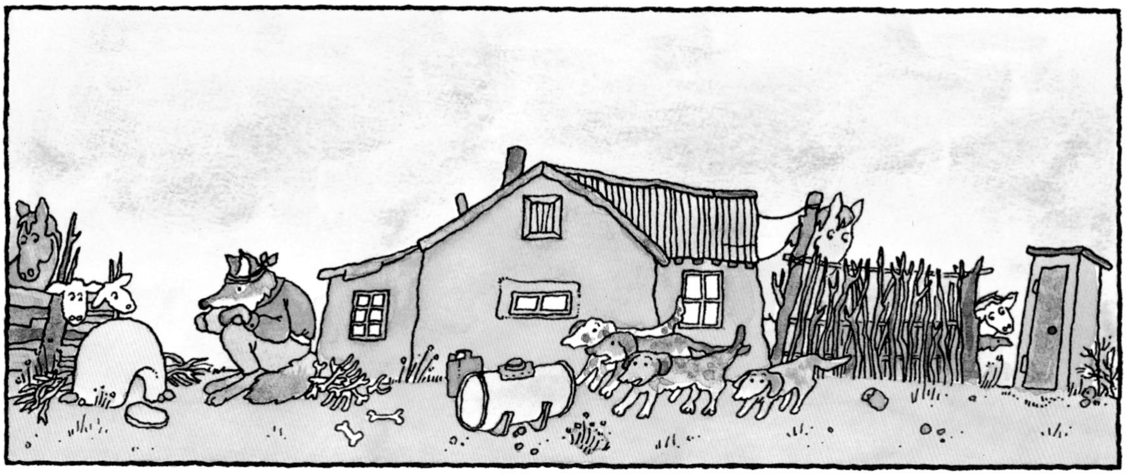

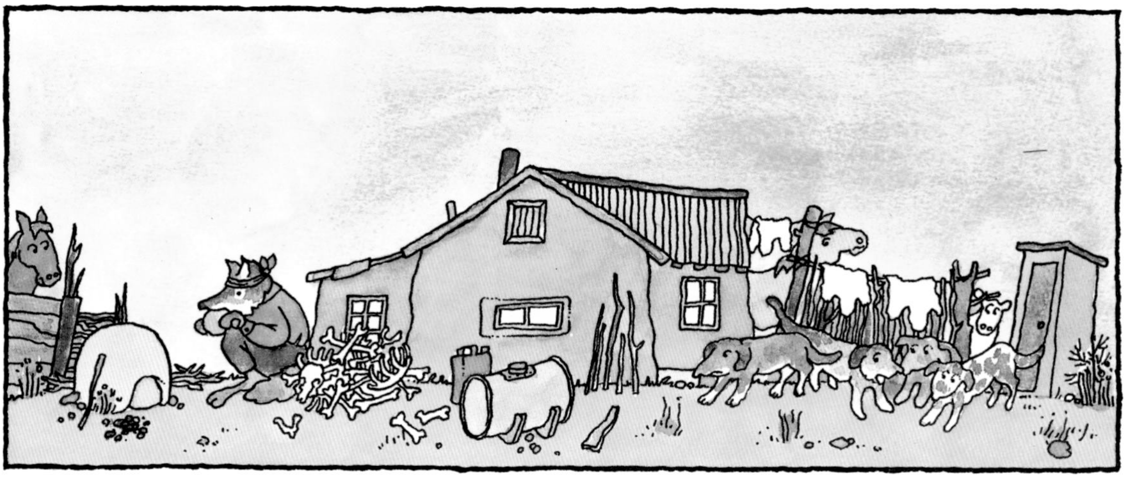

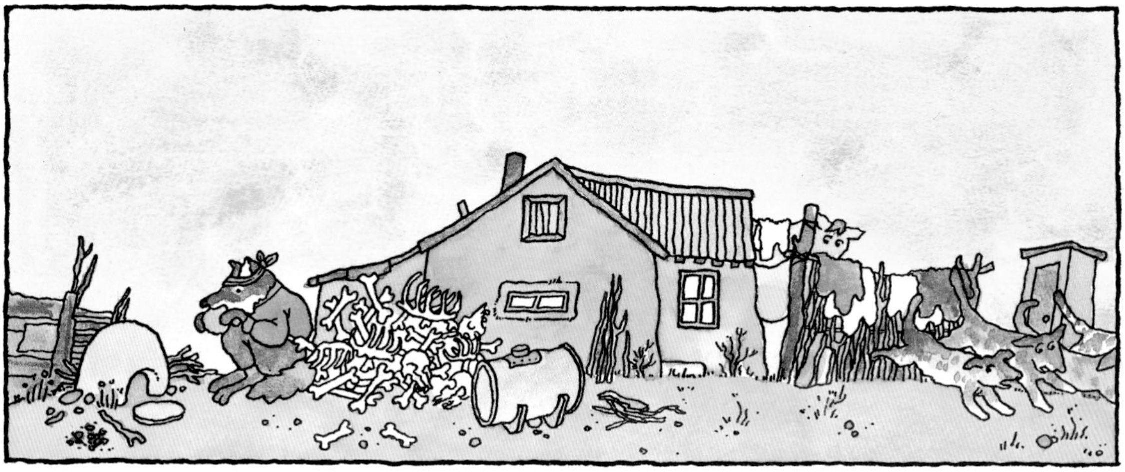

After that, Coyote lost his appetite for everything but gold. His heart was set on it. So he sold his house, his cornfield, and whatever else he had and bought gold.

He put it all together in one pile and admired it. Then he buried it in a secret place. It was as if he had buried his heart. Every day he dug it up and looked at it. It made him glad to see it. It soothed him.

But someone who knew where the gold was buried and had seen him looking at it came along one day and took it.

When Coyote saw that his gold was no more, he was wild with grief. He cried and tore his hair. He was so angry he pricked his skin with thorns and whipped himself all over.

Someone who happened to come by asked what was the matter, and Coyote told him the whole story.

Then the stranger said, "Stop crying. Settle your heart. Your gold did nothing for you. Go bury a stone where your gold was hidden, and tell yourself, 'This is my gold.' It will do you just as much good and never cause you any trouble." *And if you do have gold, you'd better keep it well hidden.*

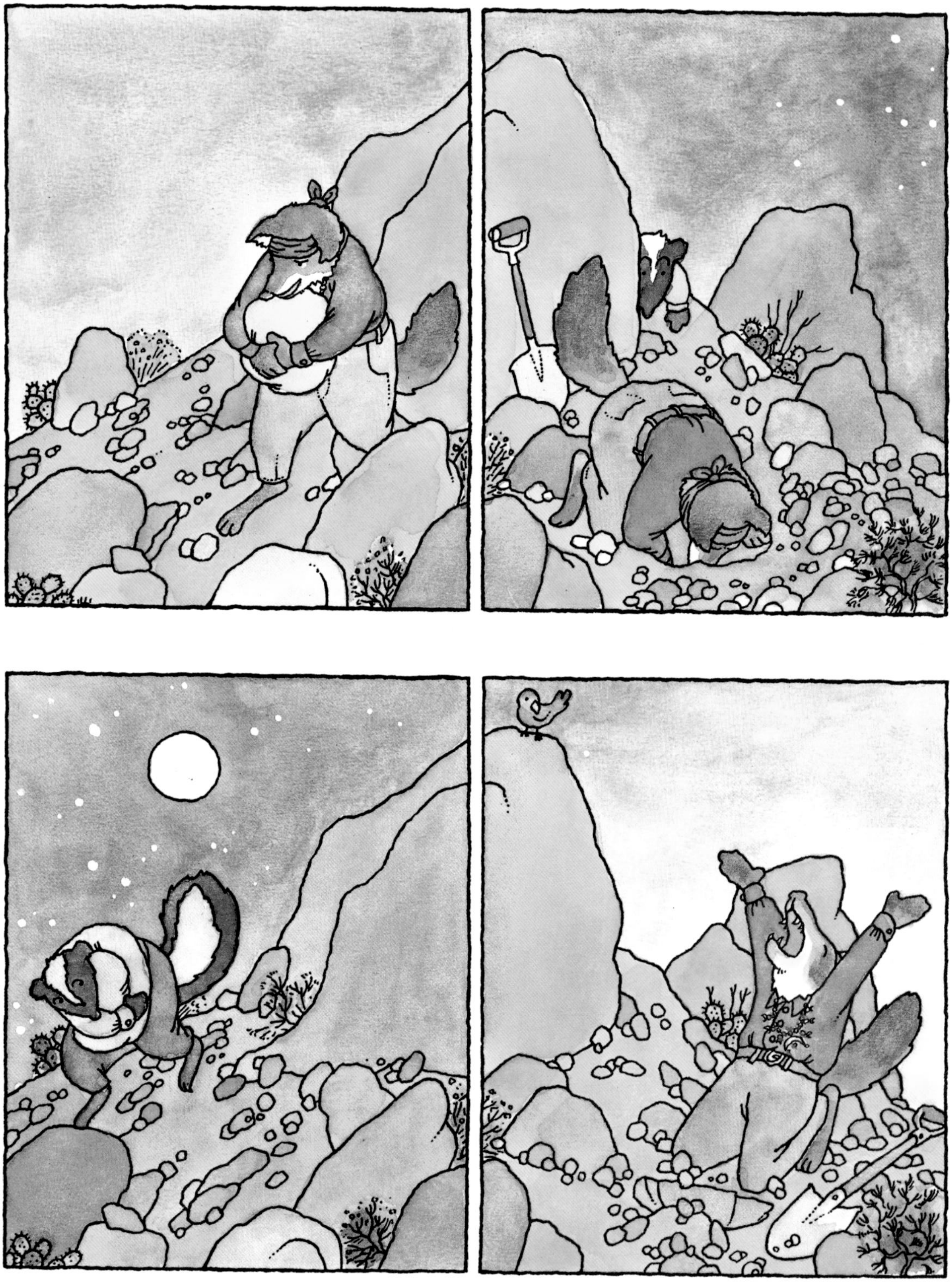

But Coyote could always find trouble. Hungry again, he went hunting for something to eat and got caught in a trap. When he pulled himself free, his tail came off.

He was ashamed. It was worrisome that he had no tail. So he called all the coyotes together and said, "Listen, my children. Why are you dragging those tails around? Who needs them? All you're doing is sweeping the dirt. Cut them off, slice them off!"

And on and on he talked. Finally a little coyote girl stepped up and gave him an answer. "Oh, father!" she said. "Be quiet! Why should we hurt ourselves just to make you look good?"

If you don't need it, don't do it.

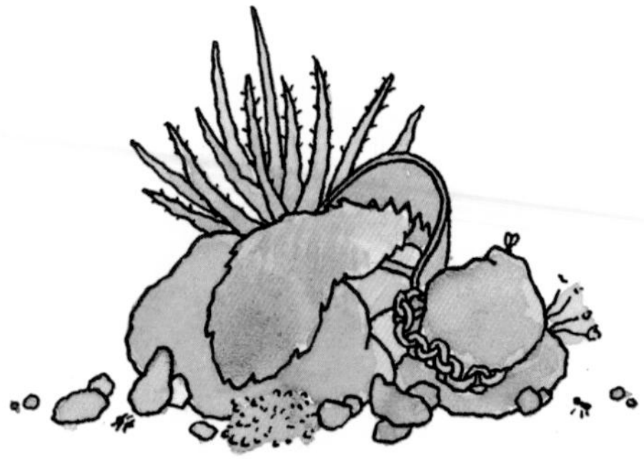

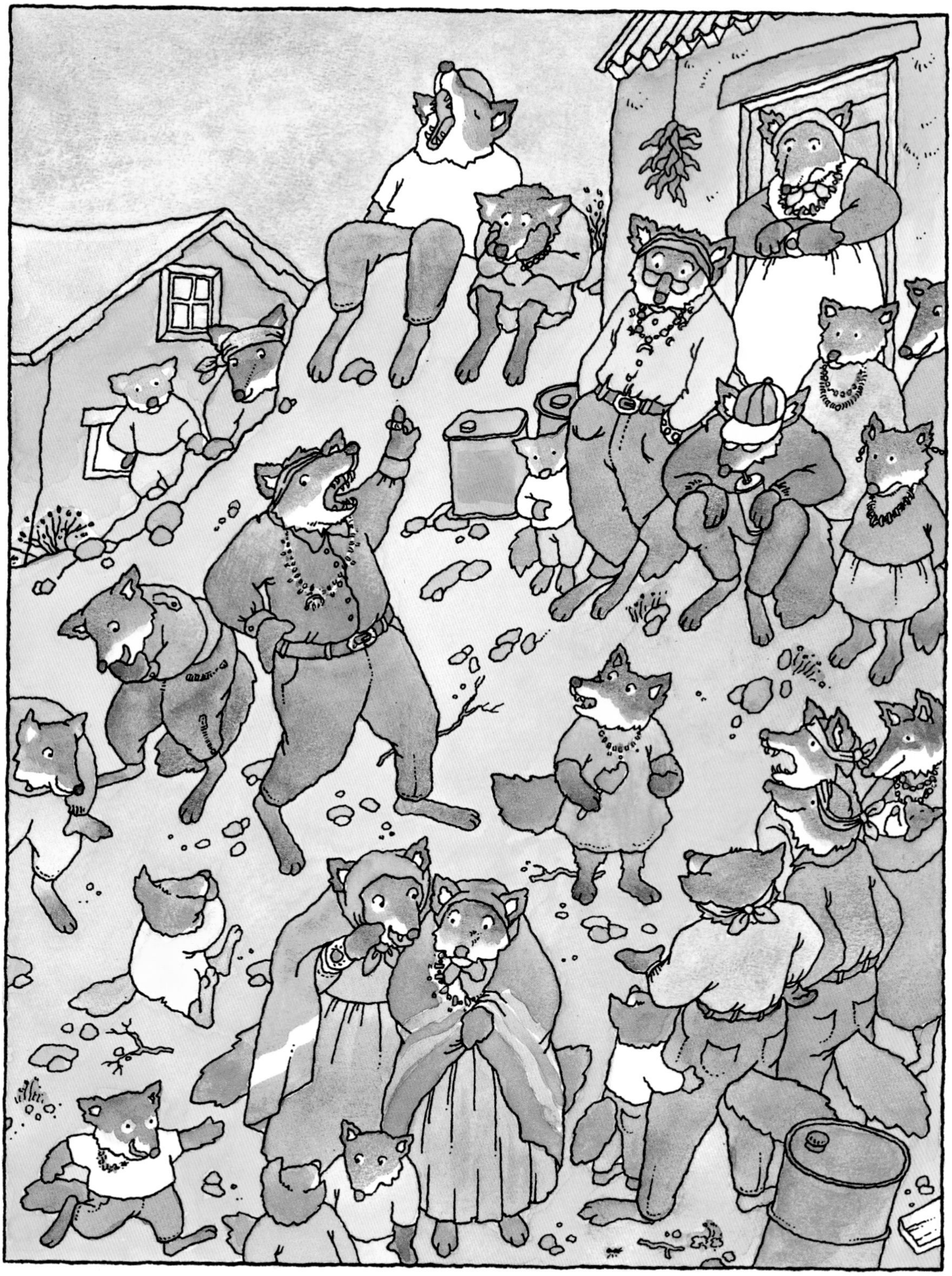

Coyote went on by himself. Not far from where he was traveling, Wolf and Rooster were coming along the same road. In those days, they say, Wolf and Rooster were friends.

Well, it got to be dark and it was time to go to sleep. So Rooster perched in the top of a tree, and Wolf stretched out in a little hollow at the tree's bottom.

In the morning when the sun came up, Rooster began to crow, as roosters do. Coyote, who had been sleeping nearby, woke up and came running over to the tree, looking for something to eat.

"What a beautiful song I'm hearing!" cried Coyote. "Come down. I want to hug you."

"Oh, good," said Rooster. "But I won't come down just yet. First you have to wake up the doorman, so there'll be somebody to open the door when I get there."

Coyote believed him and started running around the tree, thinking, "Where is the doorman?" The next thing he knew, he had stepped on Wolf. Wolf jumped up and grabbed him, and that was the end of Coyote. *It doesn't hurt to be clever, if you're too small to be anything else.*

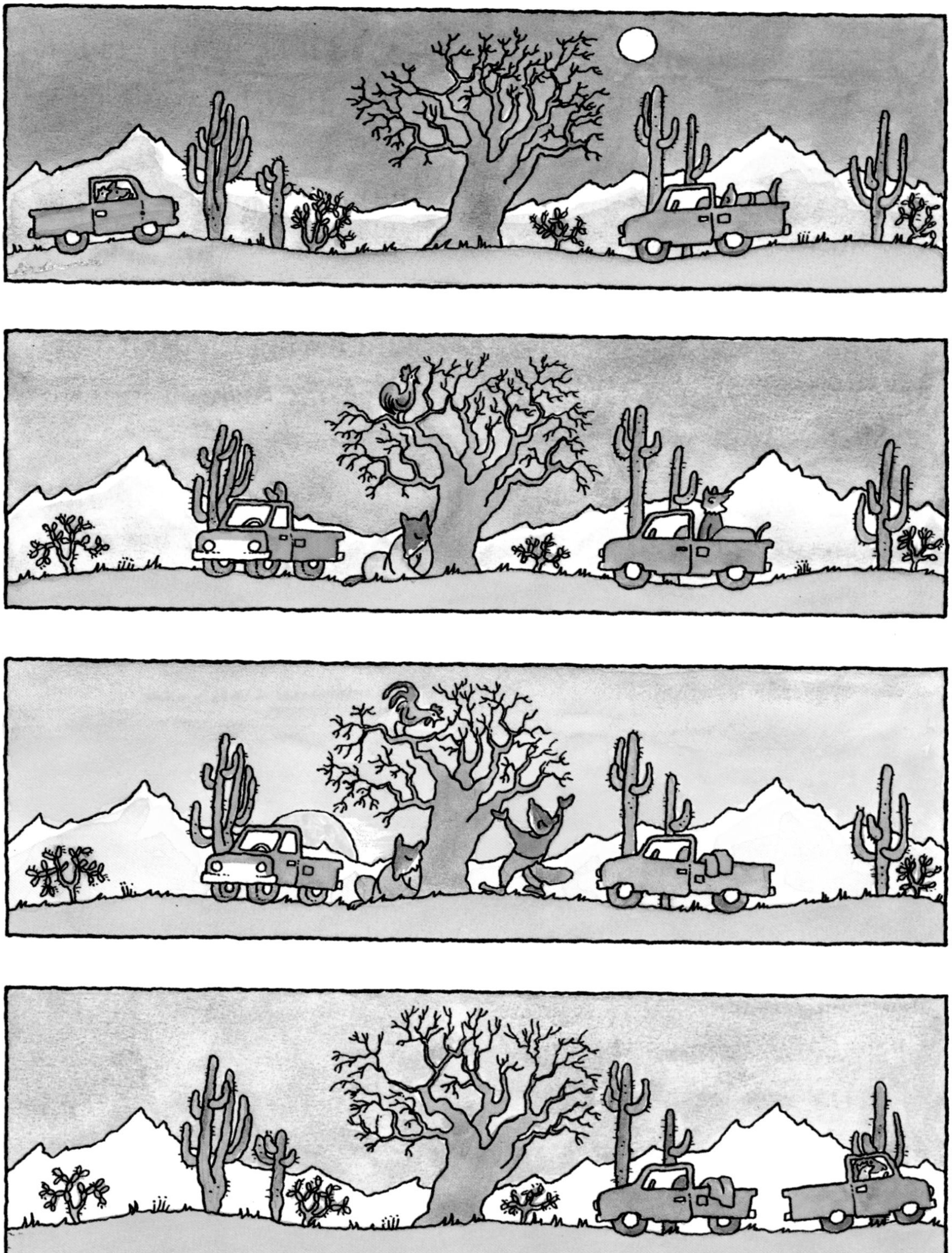

But Coyote always came back. And if he lost his tail, it grew out again. Or if he lost his house he would get a new one.

Well, one day he set himself up in the market and was answering people's questions about what would happen to them and what their future would be.

When they were all gathered around having their fortunes told, a messenger dripping with sweat came rushing into the market and said to Coyote, "Get up! How can you sit there, talking about the future, when just now Wolf has broken into your house and everything you've got is gone. Wolf has taken it all!"

Hearing this, Coyote jumped up and started for home.

As he was leaving the market, someone came up to him and said: *How can you tell people what will be done to them, if you don't know what's being done to yourself?*

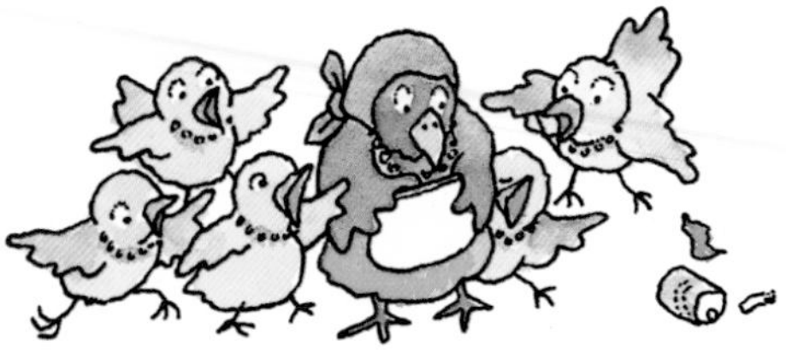

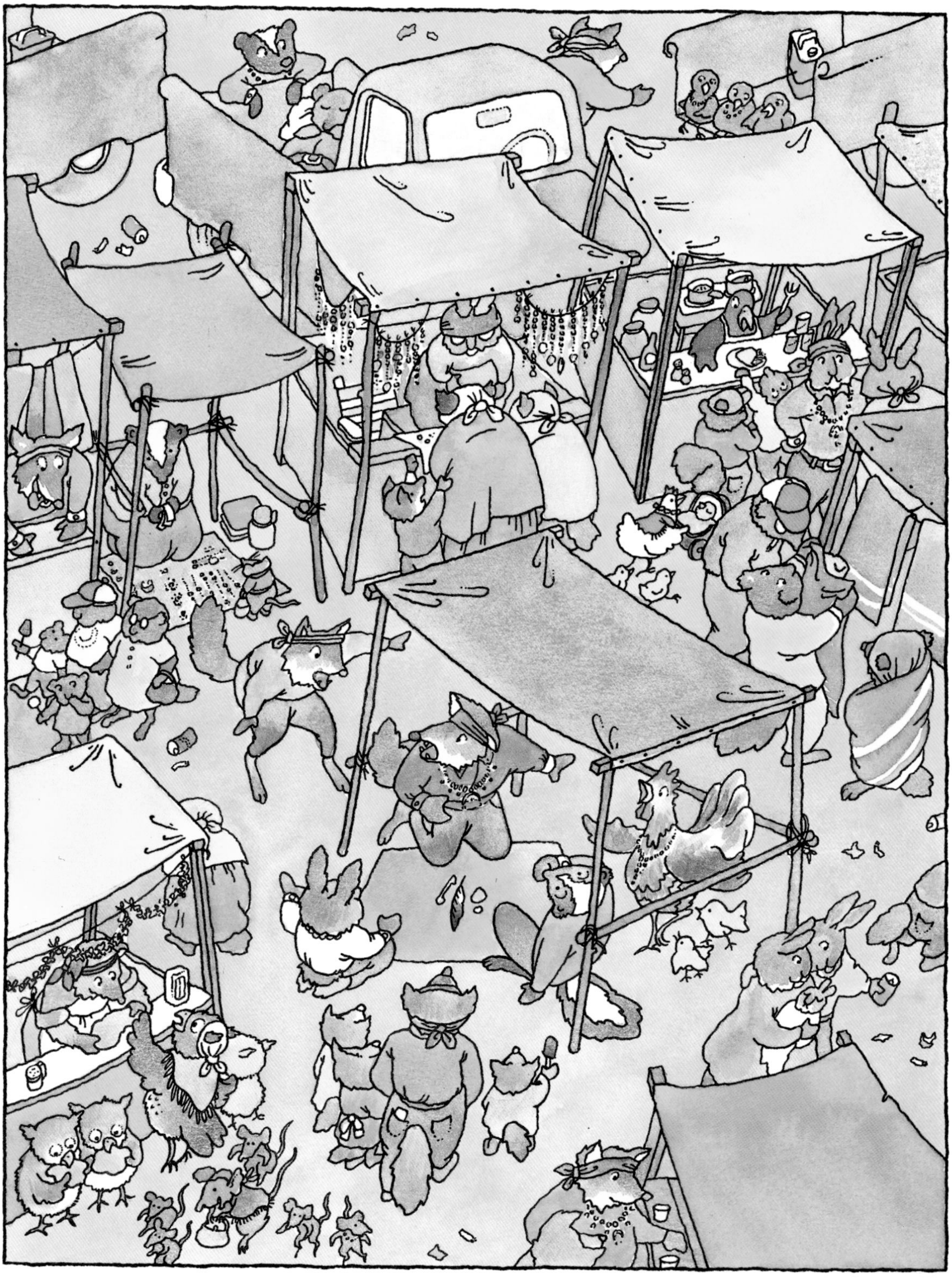

By the time Coyote got home, he was already feeling sick. The next day he was sicker still, and the day after that he was even worse. His wife tried to heal him with medicine, but she had to give up. He was too sick.

Finally he threw himself at the mercy of the gods. He prayed to them, "Cure me, gods, and I'll give you a hundred cows."

His wife overheard him and said, "If you're cured, where in the world will you get all those cows you're promising?"

"Don't be silly," said Coyote. "If I'm cured, do you think somebody's going to come down from the sky and ask me for cows?" *Promises come easily in time of need.*

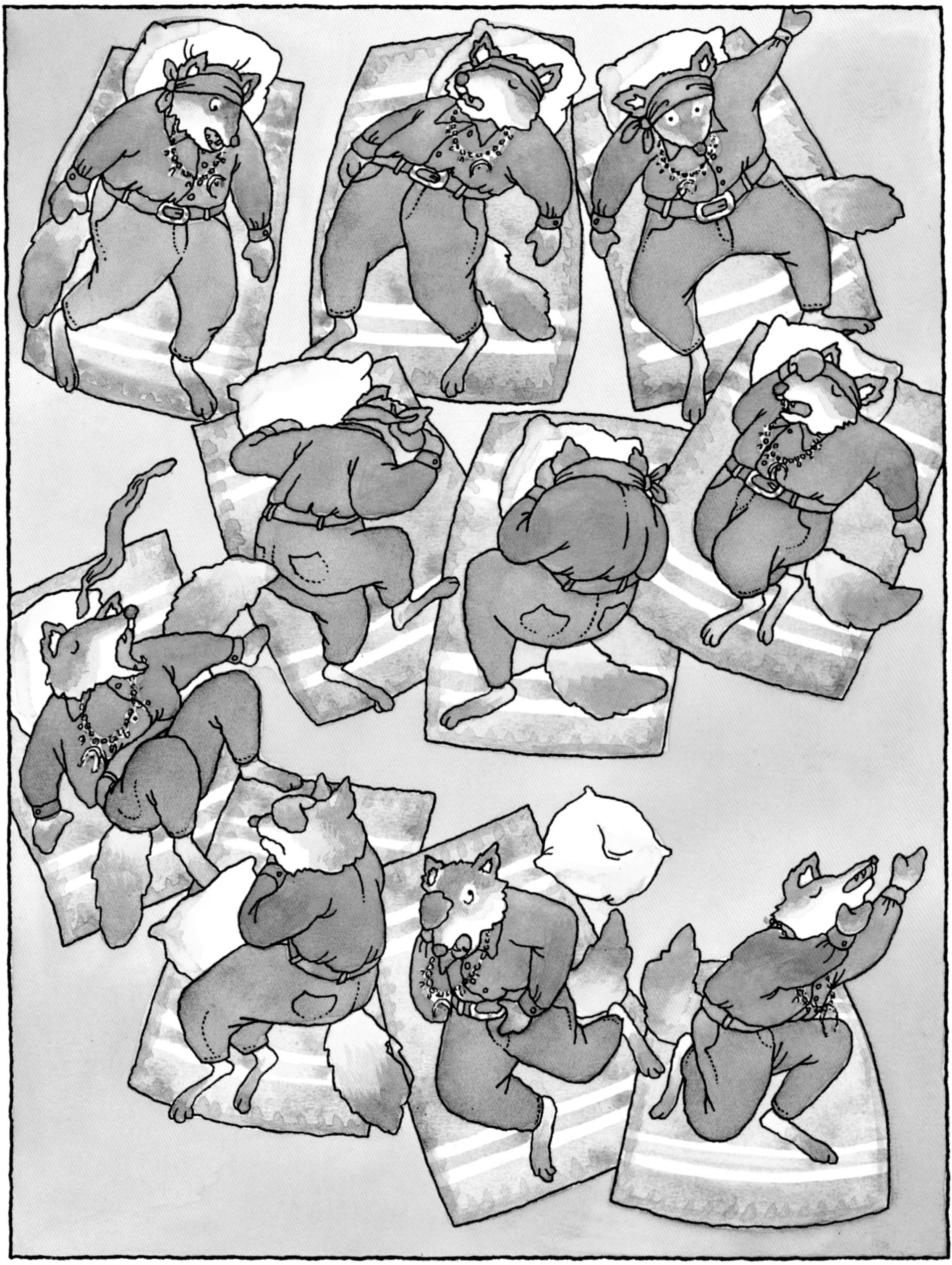

Coyote got well, but his heart was still sick. It was all because of Wolf. Coyote and Wolf, it seems, were deadly enemies. They really hated each other.

One day these two and some others went out in a boat together, and a big wind blew up. It was terrifying. The boat was about to sink.

Coyote, who was riding in the boat's behind, trying to steer it, called out to the others, "O my children! Can you see? Where is the boat sinking first?"

"The boat's nose is sinking first," they all answered.

And when Coyote, who was riding behind, heard this, he was overjoyed, because his enemy was riding in the nose.

"Ah," he said, "even if we all drown, it settles my heart to know that my enemy drowns first." *He who thinks of revenge forgets everything else.*

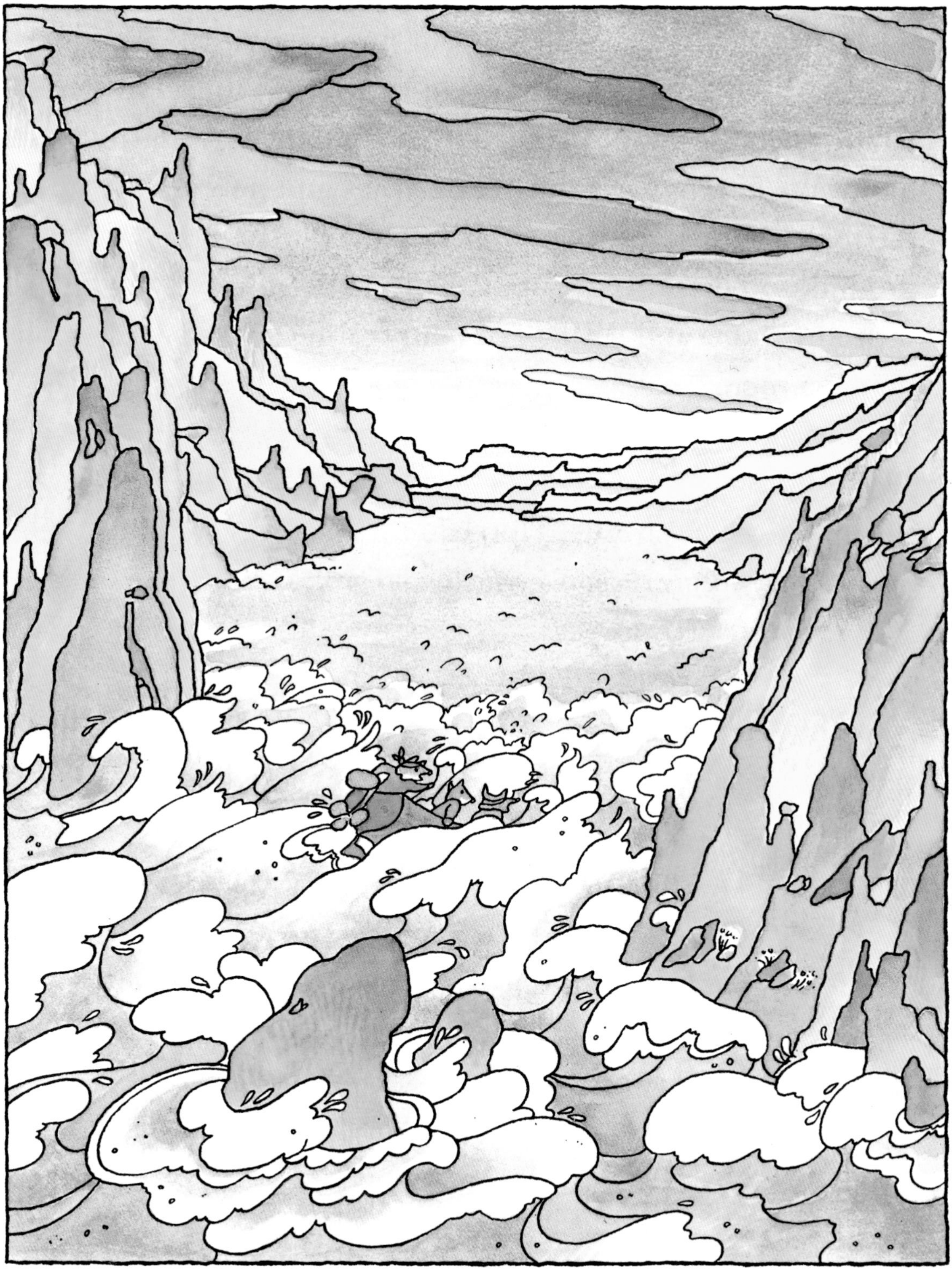

Another time, Wolf was out hunting with Puma, and all of a sudden the two of them fixed their eyes on a young fawn. Each one claimed it for himself. They started to fight over it. They grabbed each other and gave each other terrible wounds, and when at last they were lying on the ground, too dizzy to get up, Coyote came along.

Seeing Puma and Wolf all out of breath, Coyote went right between them, snatched the fawn, and ran off with it.

Puma and Wolf could do nothing but watch. They couldn't stop him.

All they could say was, "Too bad for us. We killed ourselves for Coyote." *Many there are who live off others, eat and drink the efforts of others.*

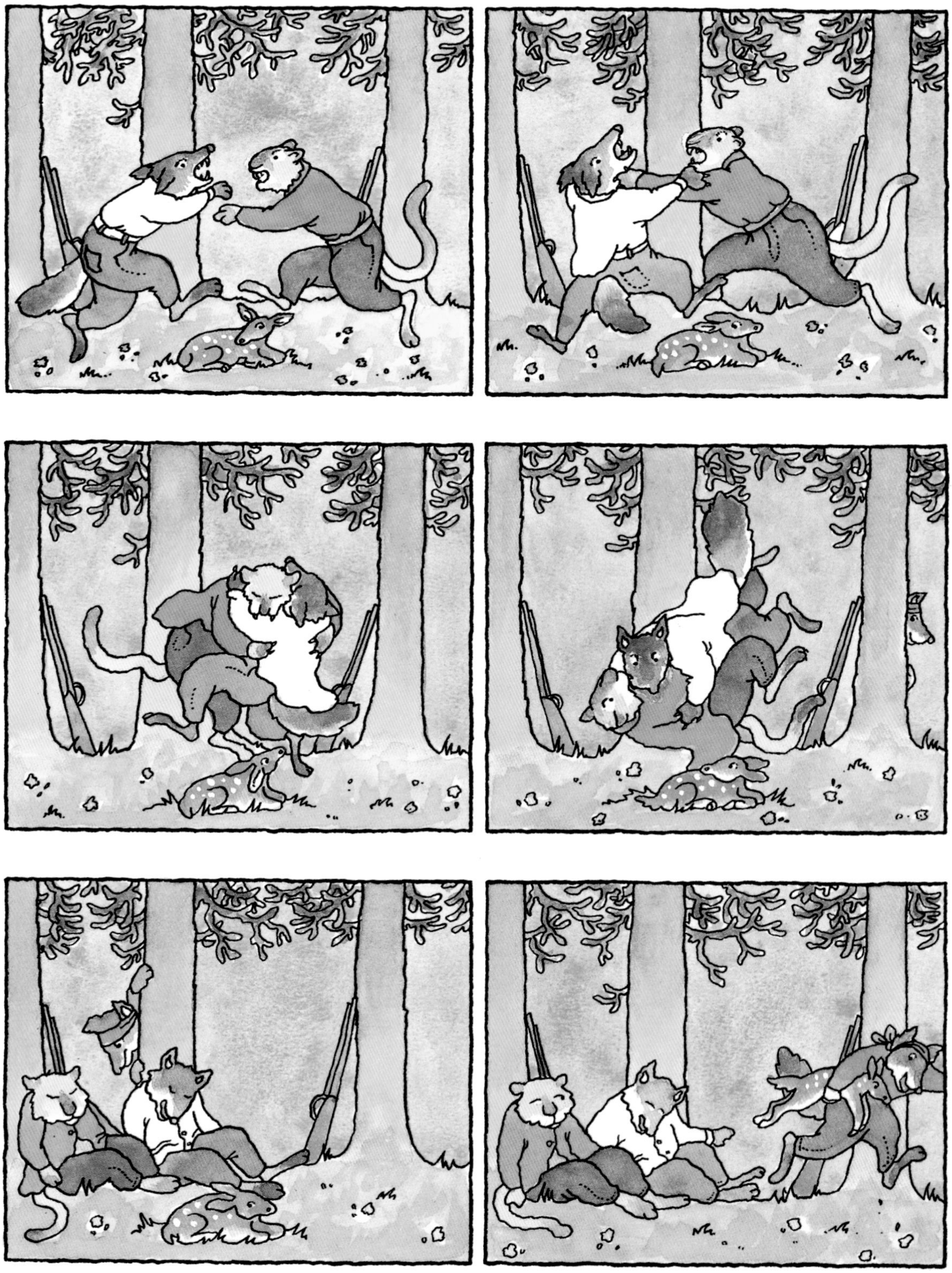

Traveling along, Coyote met White Beard, and the two of them traveled together.

When Coyote and White Beard got thirsty, they jumped into a well. They drank their fill, then White Beard began looking around to see how he could get back out.

"Don't worry," said Coyote. "I know how we can do it. Just stand up straight and put your hands against the side of the well. Lift your head so your horns stick out behind, and I'll climb on your back. As soon as I'm out, I'll reach over and pull you up."

It sounded good to White Beard. He did what he was told, and Coyote climbed on top of him. But then, when Coyote was free, he ran around the edge of the well, laughing at White Beard. White Beard was furious.

"Friend," said Coyote, "if your brain was as big as your beard, you would have thought about how to get out before you jumped in." *The truth hits hardest when it's too late to complain.*

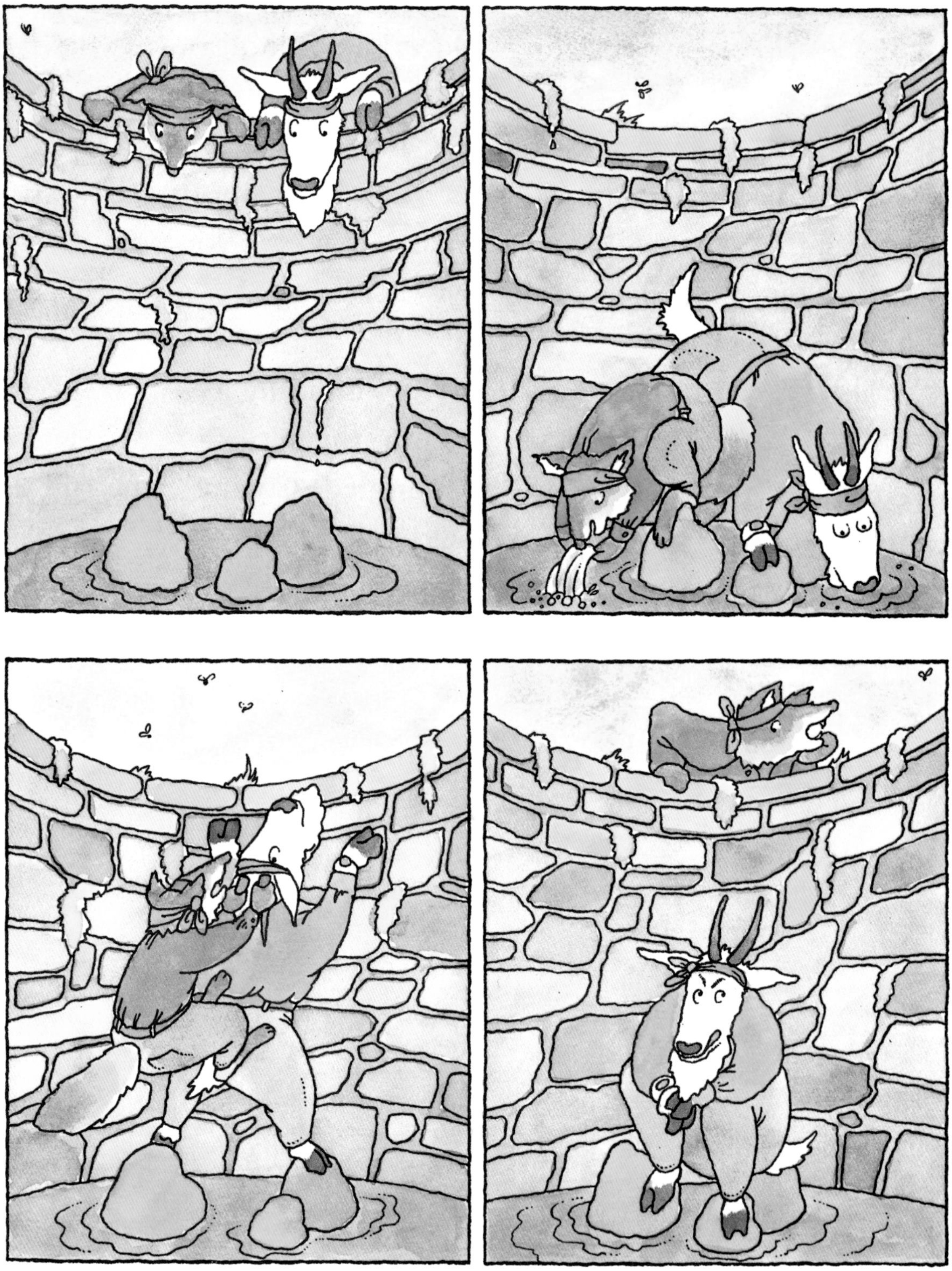

Coyote kept traveling. When he got hungry, he would catch birds.

One time, when he had spread his net under the trees, a blackbird perched overhead started worrying about what was happening. It came down and said, "What are you doing?"

"I'm building a city," said Coyote, and he left his net and hid behind a tree.

The blackbird said to itself, "If he's building a city, let's see what it's like." Then it flew right into the net.

As soon as the blackbird was tangled, Coyote came running out from behind the tree and grabbed it.

"Oh, bird catcher!" said the blackbird. "If this is how you build a city, who would want to live there?" *This fable shows us how the powerful can hurt the weak.*

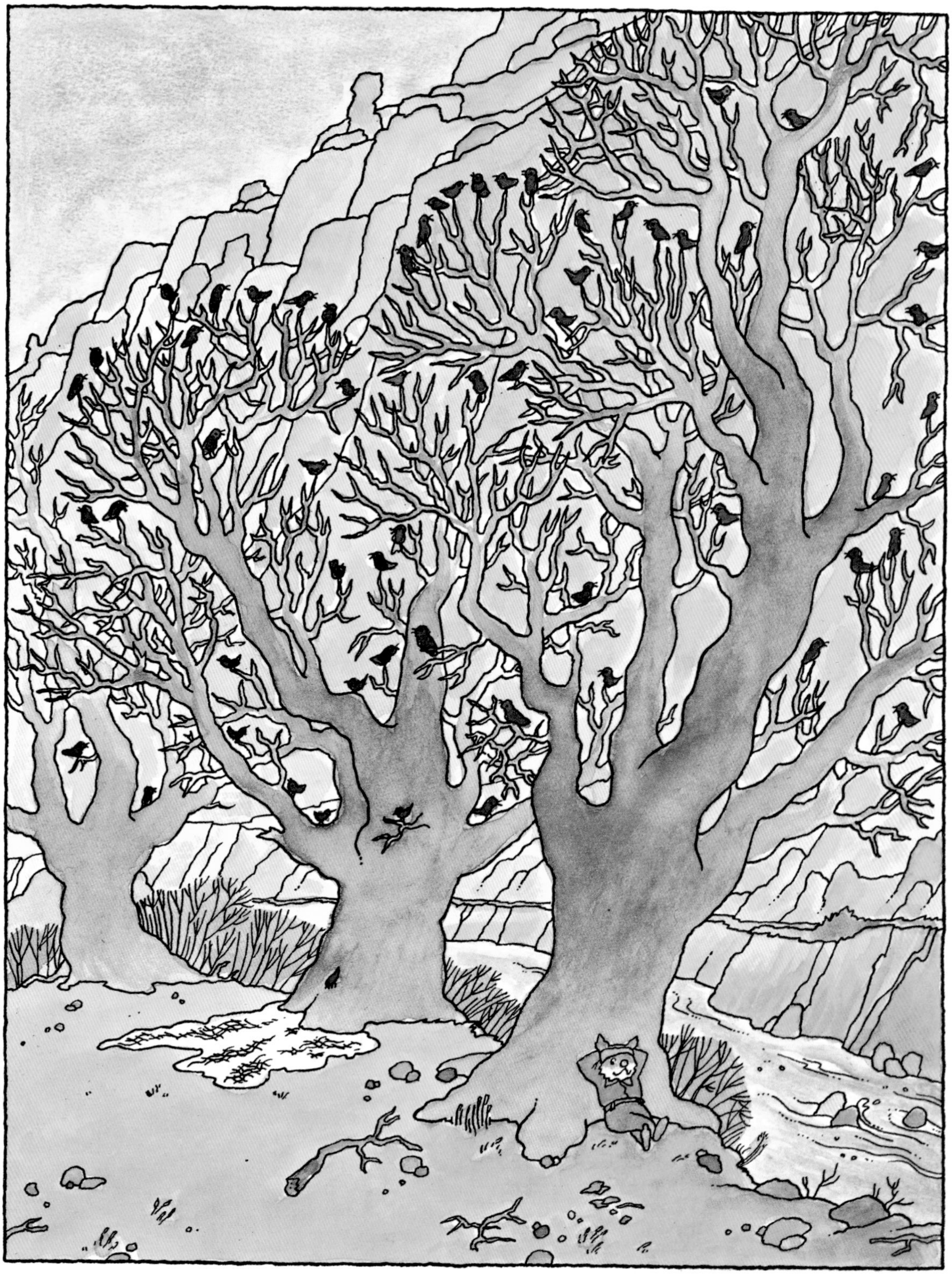

Coyote kept on traveling until he got to a place where nobody knew who he was. Then he set himself up as a doctor.

Now, there was a little old blind woman living in that place, and when she heard there was a doctor, she called him and told him to cure her. Well, the first thing they talked about was how she would pay him. As soon as her eyes were healed, they decided, she would give him his money.

Then he started to work the cure. He rubbed her eyes with cold-stone weed, and when the treatment was finished, she lay down and stretched herself out on her cot. There in the dark he left her.

But while he was leaving, he secretly took whatever he saw that the little old woman had. Her blankets, her bowls, everything.

When her eyes got well, the little old woman looked around and saw that there was nothing left in her house. Then here comes the doctor to ask for his money. "O princess," he says, "give me my money. Don't forget, I cured your eyes."

"My darling, what do you mean?" she replied. "You say you cured me? Before you were here, I used to find all sorts of things in my house. And now I see nothing at all." *The bad you do can turn around and shame you.*

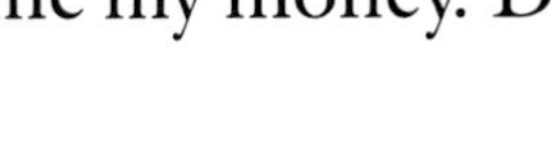

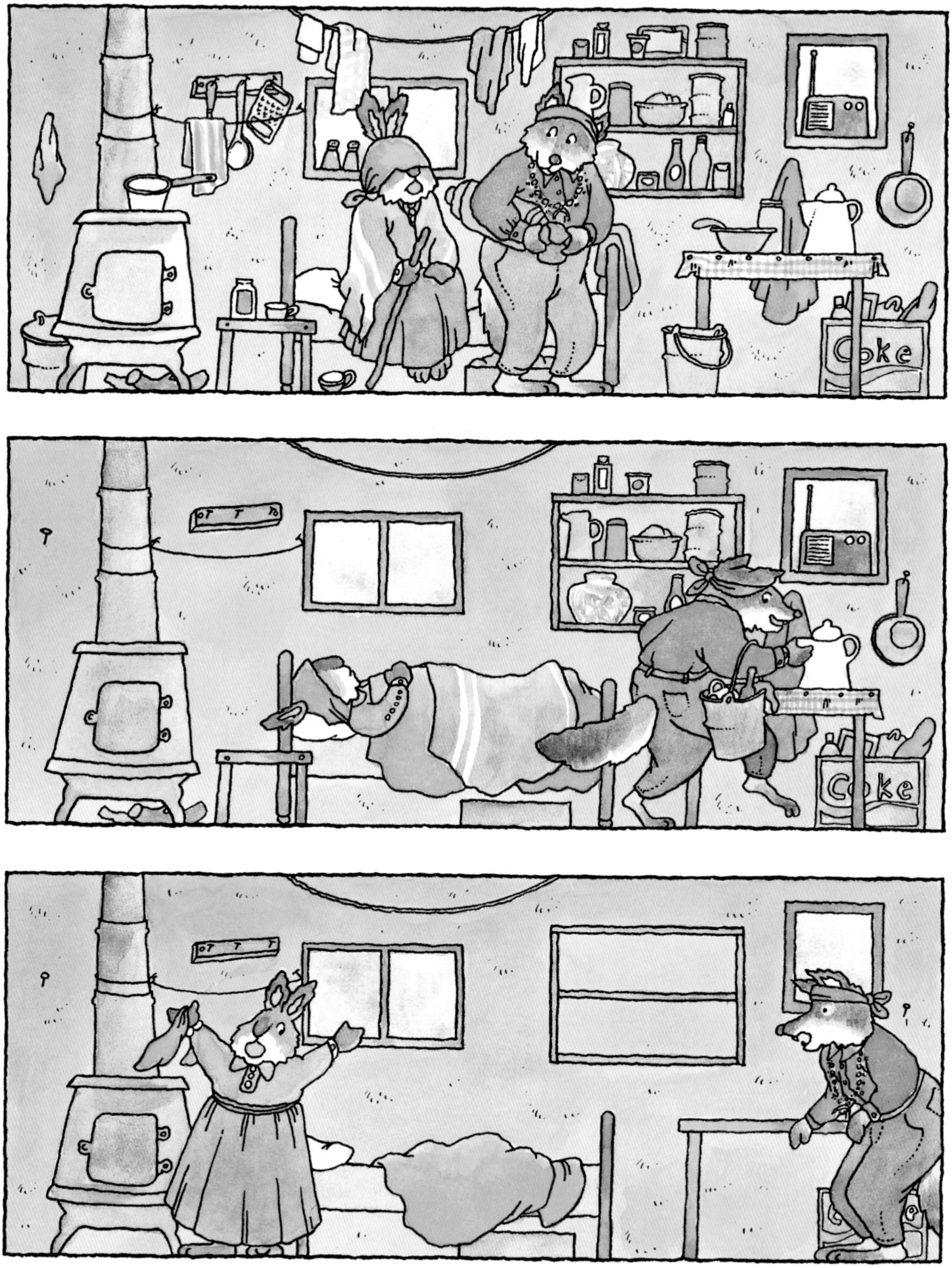
Coke
Coke

Coyote had another patient, and in the morning he would go see him to ask how he had been during the night.

"I had hot sweats," said the patient one morning.

"That's fine," said Coyote.

The next day he came back and asked the same question: "How were you during the night?"

"I had cold chills all night."

"Excellent!" said the doctor.

And a third time Coyote comes and asks the patient how he feels. This time he can see that the patient is all swollen and in great pain.

"Ah, that's just fine," he says.

And after Coyote had left, one of the patient's friends came to see him and asked, "How are you doing?"

"The doctor says I'm doing fine. But he himself does nothing, and now I'm worse than ever." *Sweet words are not always welcome.*

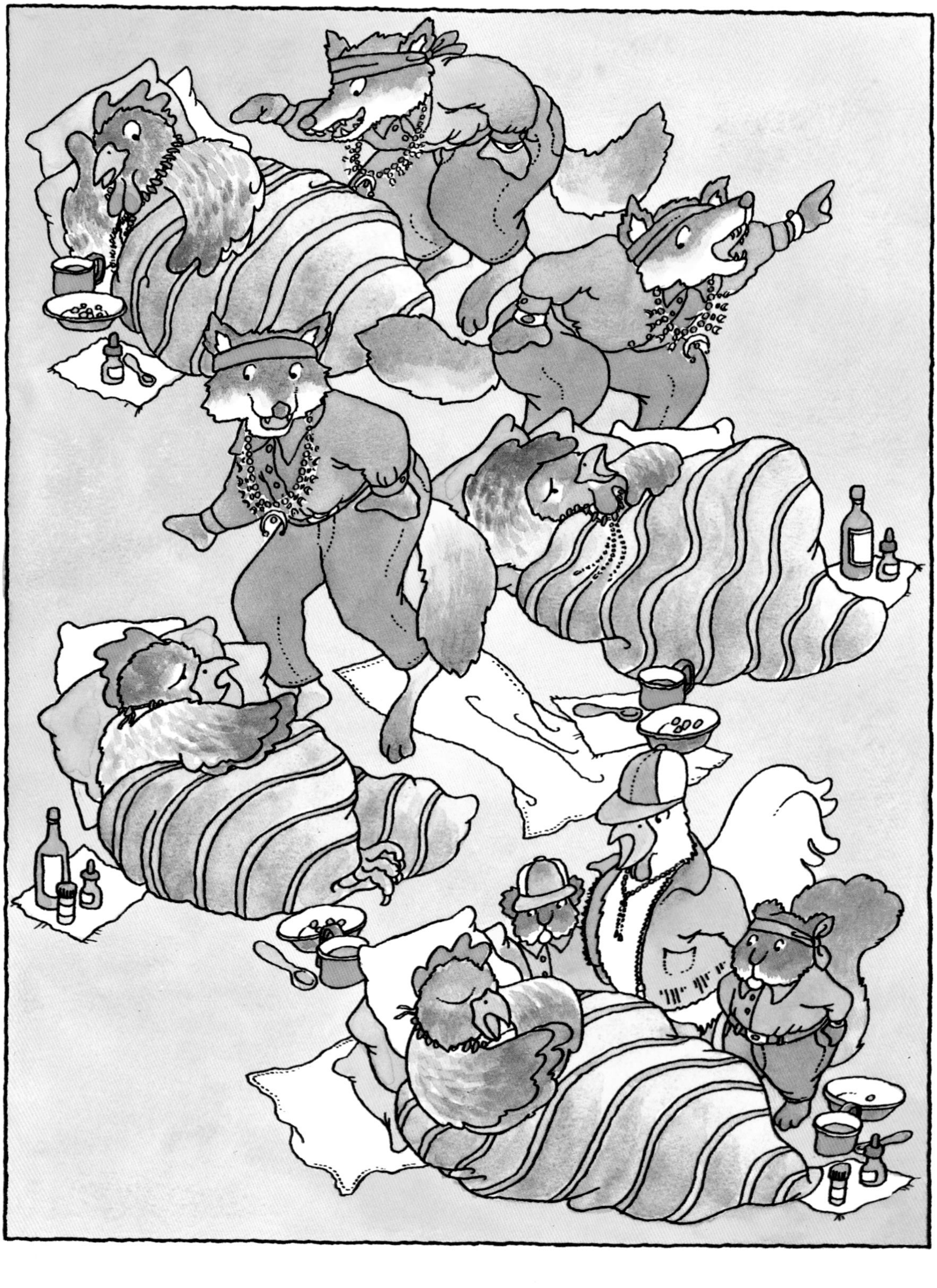

When the patient was dead, his body was carried off to the graveyard, and Coyote trotted along beside the coffin, giving advice.

"This patient," he said, "should have been drinking wine. If only he'd done it! It would have freshened his stomach, it would have cleaned out his system. He would have been cured."

"Hush!" said one of the friends who was carrying the coffin. "You should have cured him when he was still alive. Why talk now?" *Who needs the helper who helps too late?*

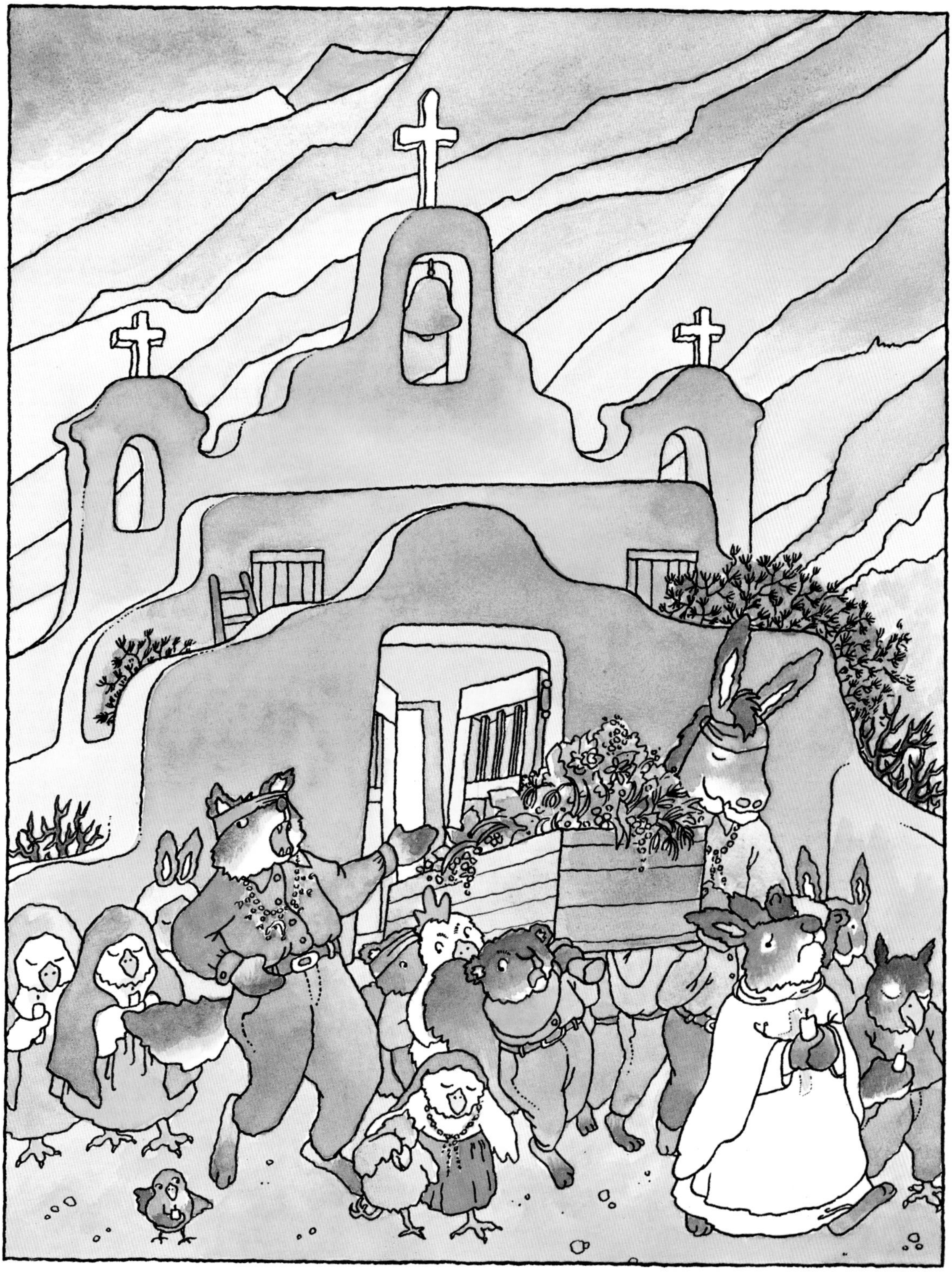

Another time, old man Puma lay sick in his cave, and all the animals were visiting him. Except Coyote.

When Wolf saw that Coyote had not come, he thought he would stir up trouble. So he said to Puma, "Look around you, king. Coyote thinks he's too important to make this visit. He doesn't even care that you're sick."

Just then Coyote arrived and heard a little of what Wolf was saying. And when Puma saw him, he bared his teeth and said, "Where were you, you rascal?"

"Hear me in peace, O lord," said Coyote. "Probably you thought nobody cared enough to do something about your illness. But I was running everywhere, looking for a cure. At last I found a medicine woman who told me just the thing that would make you well. That's why I didn't come sooner."

"And what is it?" said Puma.

"A live wolf has to be skinned," said Coyote, "and the skin has to be given to you still warm. That's what will cure you. You will feel young again."

And when Puma had ordered Wolf to be skinned, Coyote went dancing up to Wolf's fur and said, "You thought you would do a good one by stirring up the king. But did you know that you yourself would be the one to calm him down?" *When someone angry makes up evil words against another, those words come back to bite him.*

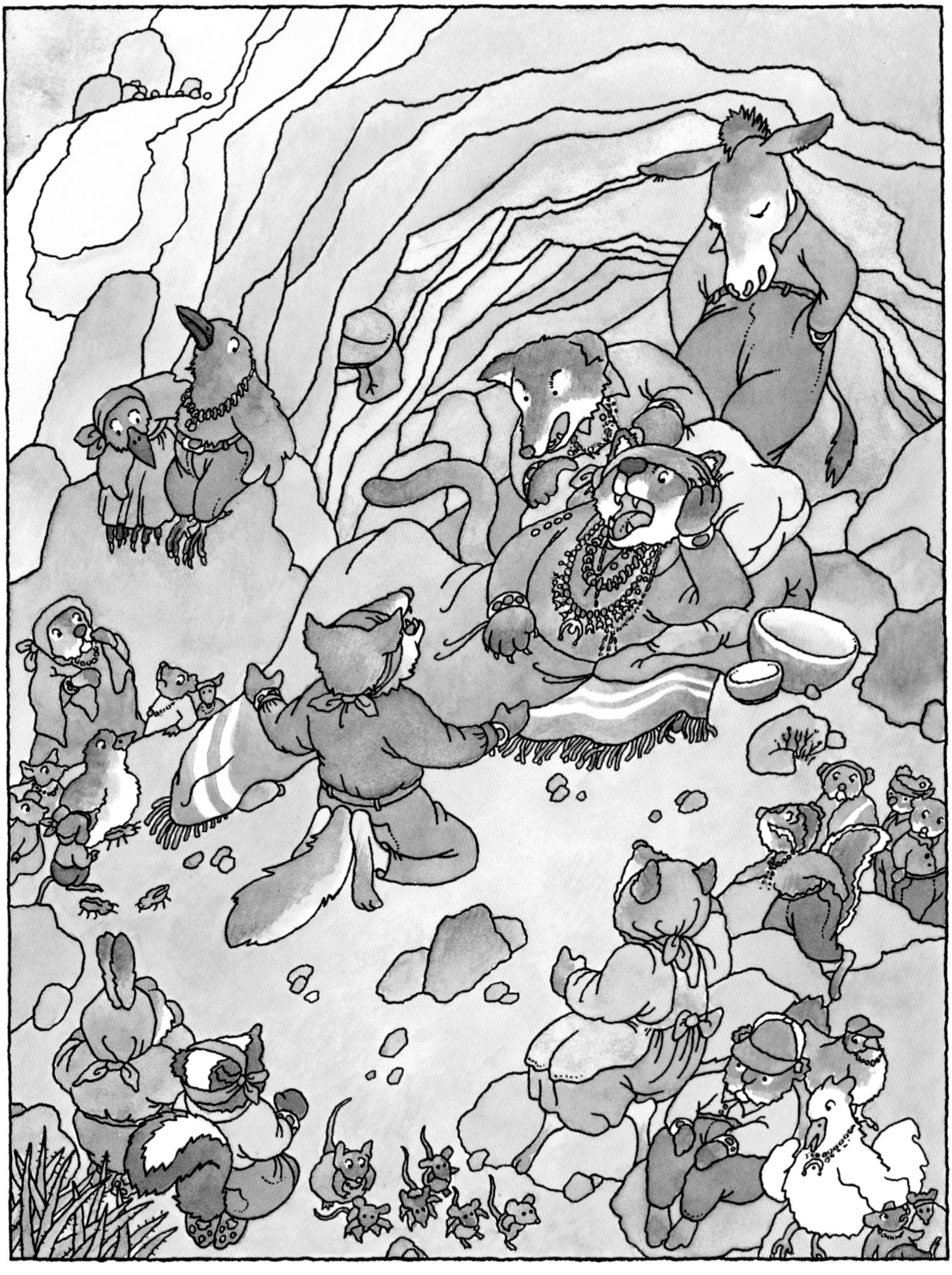

After that, Coyote went hunting with Puma, and sometimes Donkey would come along too.

One day, when all three had been hunting together and the catch was piled up, Puma told Donkey to divide it.

Poor Donkey. His mind was nowhere. He divided the catch into three piles, thinking everybody would have the same.

Puma flew into a rage. He took hold of Donkey and tore him apart. After he had eaten him, he turned to Coyote and said, "Divide the catch!"

Now, Coyote put everything together in one pile, setting just the tiniest amount to one side. Then this is what he proposed: "Here, my lord, all this is for your own good self. All for you. I'll take only these few little bits. After all, you're the one who did the most hunting."

When Puma saw this, he said, "Well done, Coyote! What taught you to be so intelligent?"

"My lord," said Coyote, "it was what happened to the donkey." *Others' mistakes teach lessons not to be missed.*

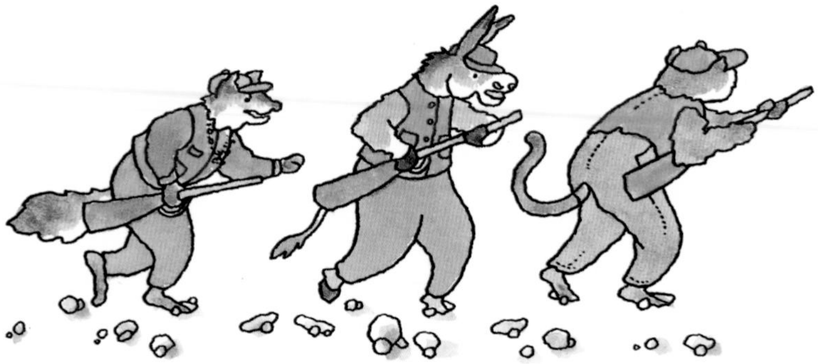

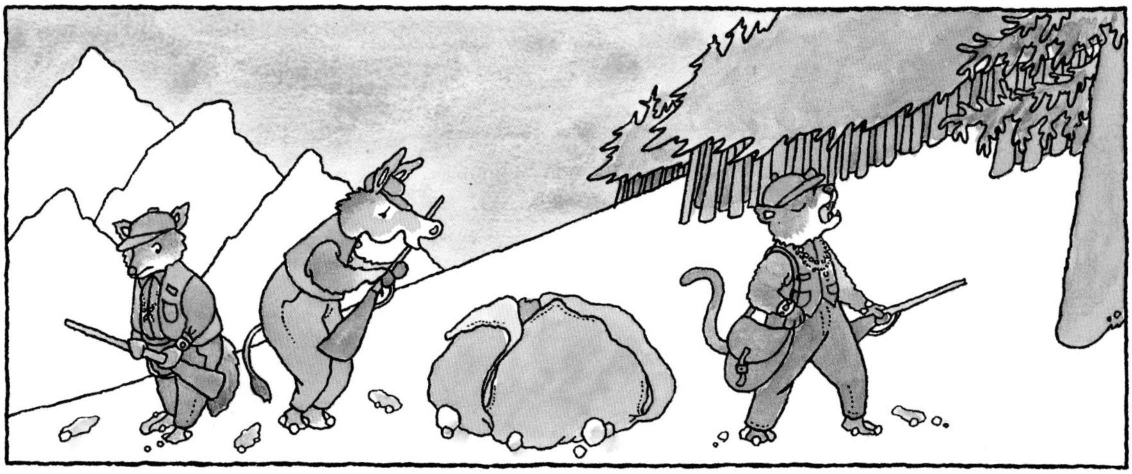
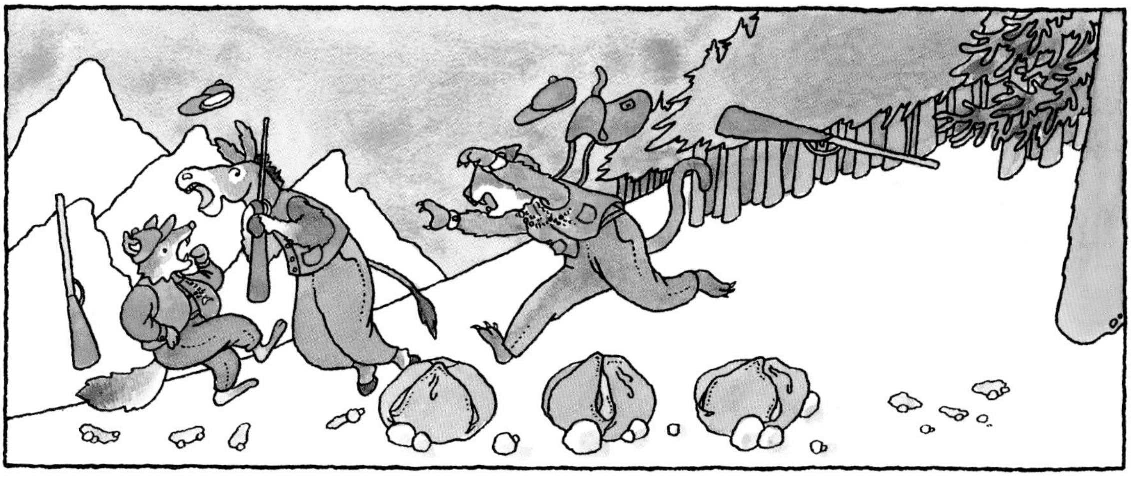
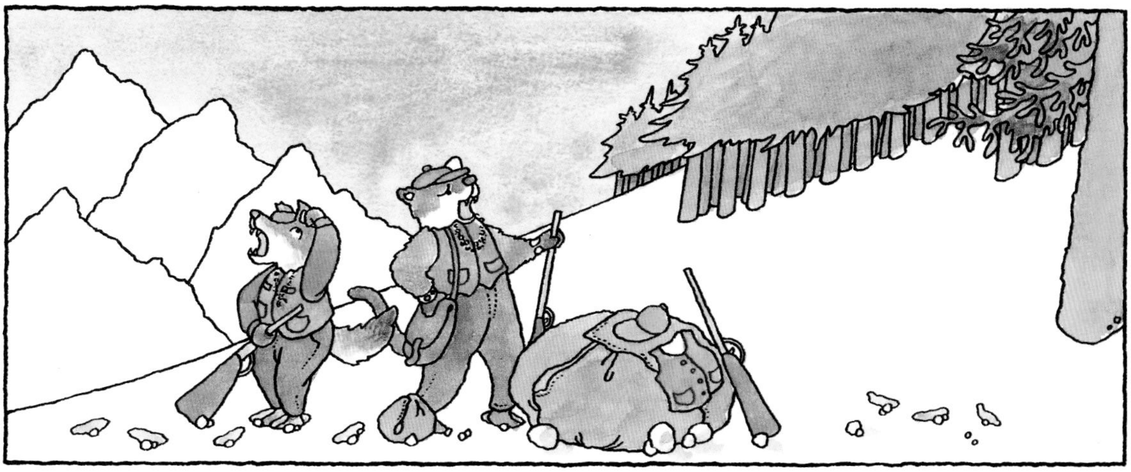

Coyote did not go hunting with Puma again. He stayed home and tended his sheep, and one day while he was grazing them at the edge of the ocean, he noticed that the water was suddenly calm. It was completely still. Then the ocean said to him, "You must sell your sheep and become a merchant."

So Coyote sold his sheep and bought dates. Then he settled himself in a ship.

When he was out on the water, a storm came up, and the ship was about to sink. So he threw the dates overboard, and they were all swallowed up in the waves. The ship sank anyway, and Coyote was just barely able to swim to shore.

And once, much later, when he was walking beside the ocean with one of his sons, the son said, "Look! The ocean is suddenly still."

Coyote laughed and said, "I know what the ocean wants, for it is a clever one. It wants to eat more dates." *An injury done once warns, "Never again."*

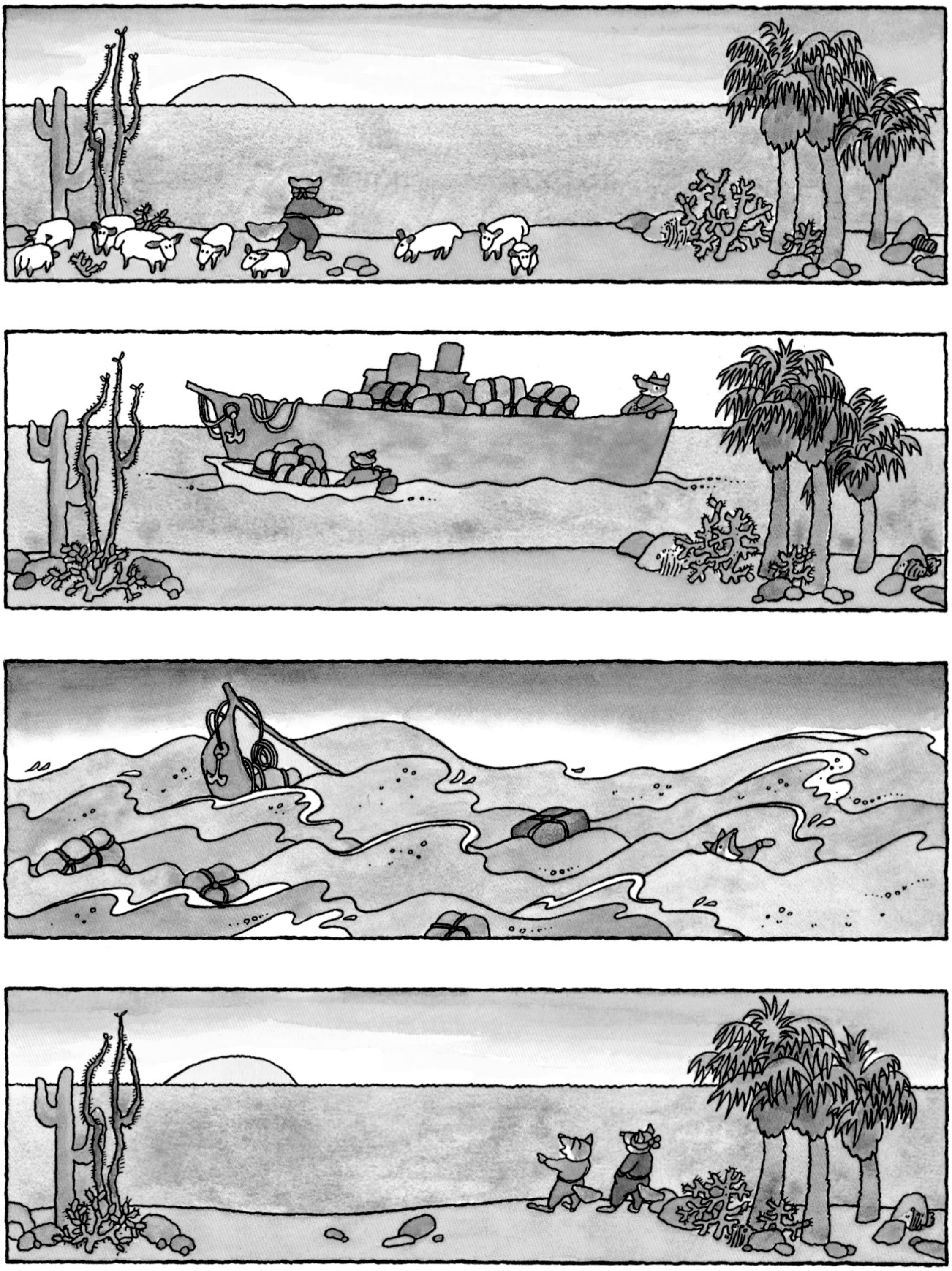

The older he got, the smarter he was, and it got to be harder to fool him. Once, they say, he fell in with a crocodile. Well, it's a kind of water monster with legs, like a lizard. It scares everybody. It's terribly ugly.

Then it started to brag about its important ancestors, and it couldn't stop talking. It told stories about its grandfather and its great-grandfather and its great-great-grandfather, how rich they were, and how famous.

But when its boasting words had touched on many things, Coyote said, "Words are not needed. We can tell who you are just by looking at you." *The taller the tale, the harder it falls.*

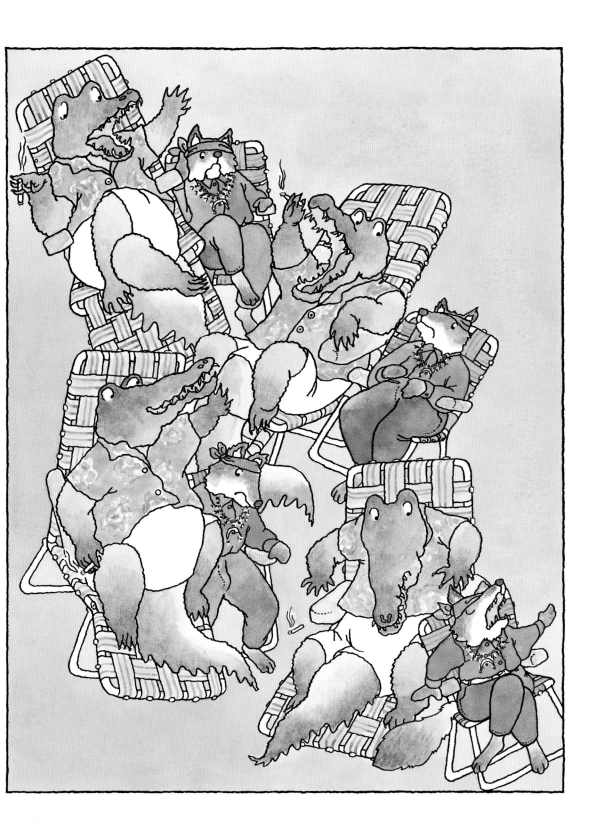

Another time, Coyote went to visit a sculptor. After he had looked around and admired some of the statues, he noticed a woman standing there. She was magnificent. Very beautiful.

So he talked to her and patted her gently with his hand. But when he saw that she couldn't speak and couldn't move, he turned to the sculptor and said, "Hah! You call this beautiful? There's not a brain in her head!" *Good looks don't make the person.*

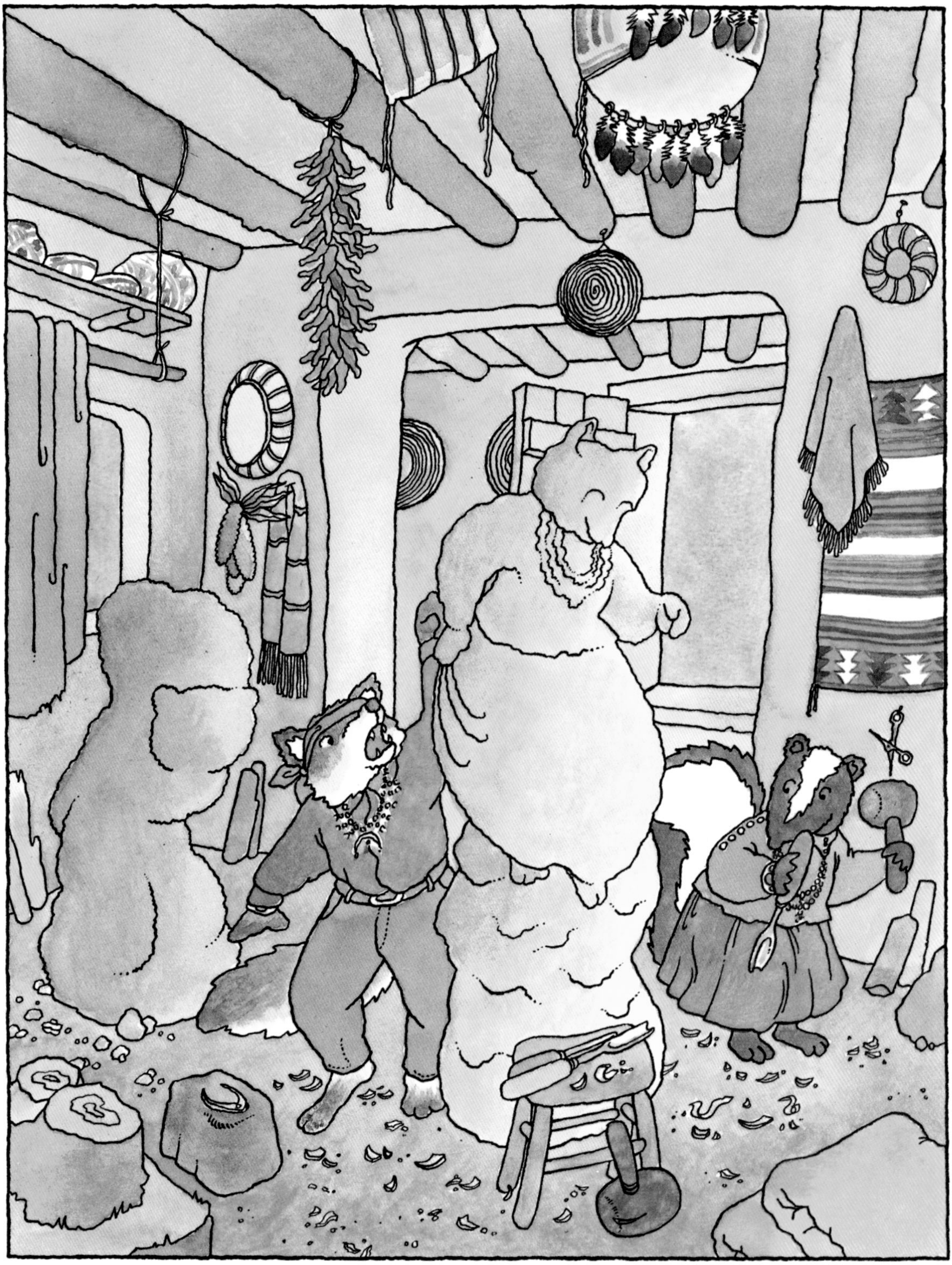

One day a dog came into the kitchen while Coyote was busy cooking and ran off with a sheep's heart in its teeth.

When Coyote saw what had happened, he said, "All right, take it! That's what you were born to do. You know that when I hear your voice again, I'll take care of you and protect you. Did you steal my heart? You have given it back to me many times over." *When we lose something, it sometimes makes us see that we are luckier than we thought.*

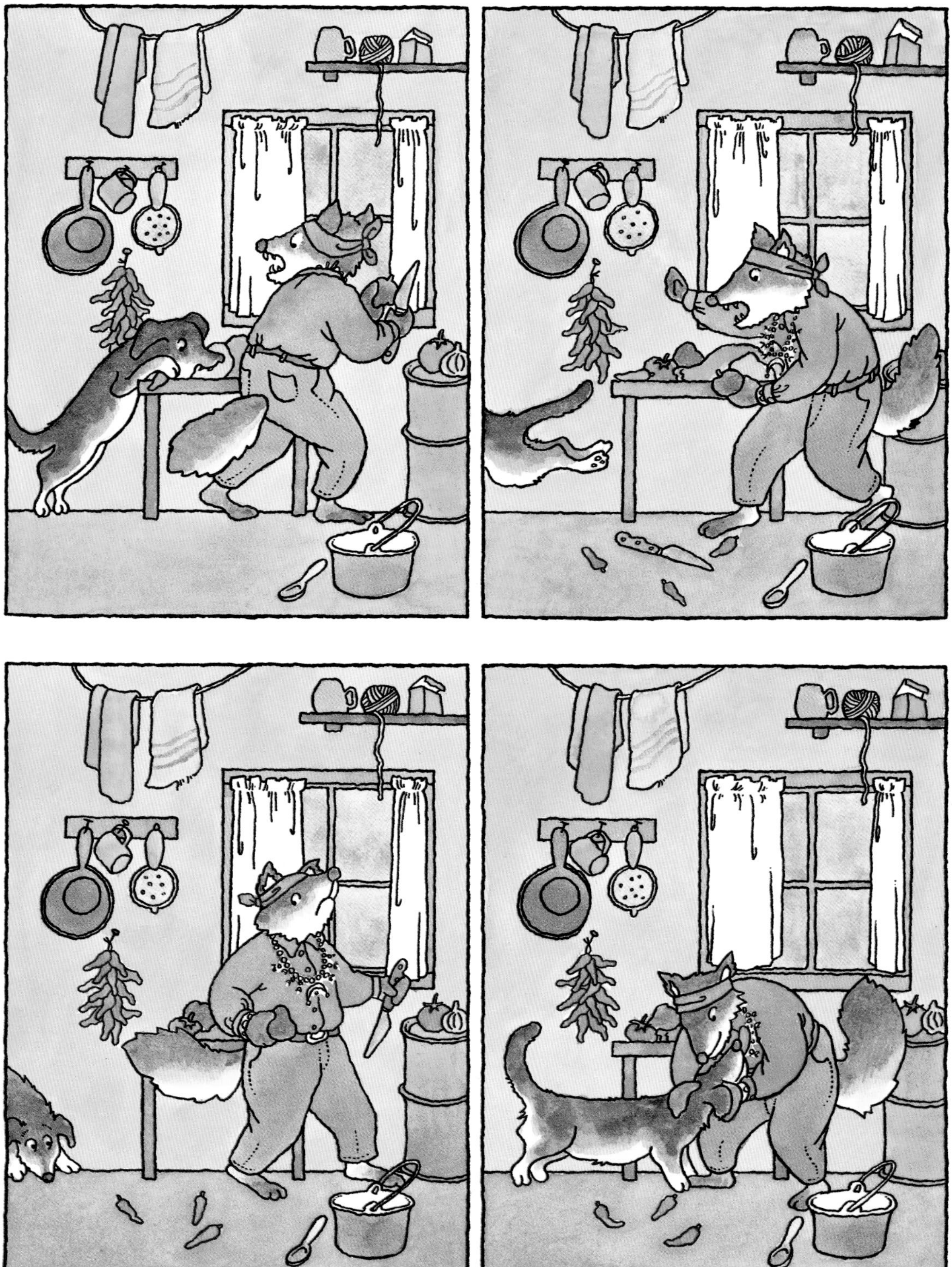

When Coyote was an old man, and the end was near, he called his sons to his bedside. Since he had nothing else to leave them, he wanted to inspire them to take care of his cornfield, so they would always have plenty to eat.

"My sons," he said, "you see how I am. Now, I want you to know that whatever I have is to be divided equally among you. Go out to the cornfield, and there you will find it."

When Coyote had passed away, his sons ran to the cornfield, thinking their father had buried his gold there. They picked up their digging sticks and worked the field from one end to the other.

They found no gold. But the field had never been worked so well before. When the ears were ripe, they had more than enough, and they were never hungry from that time on. *Great pains and much care turn into true riches.*

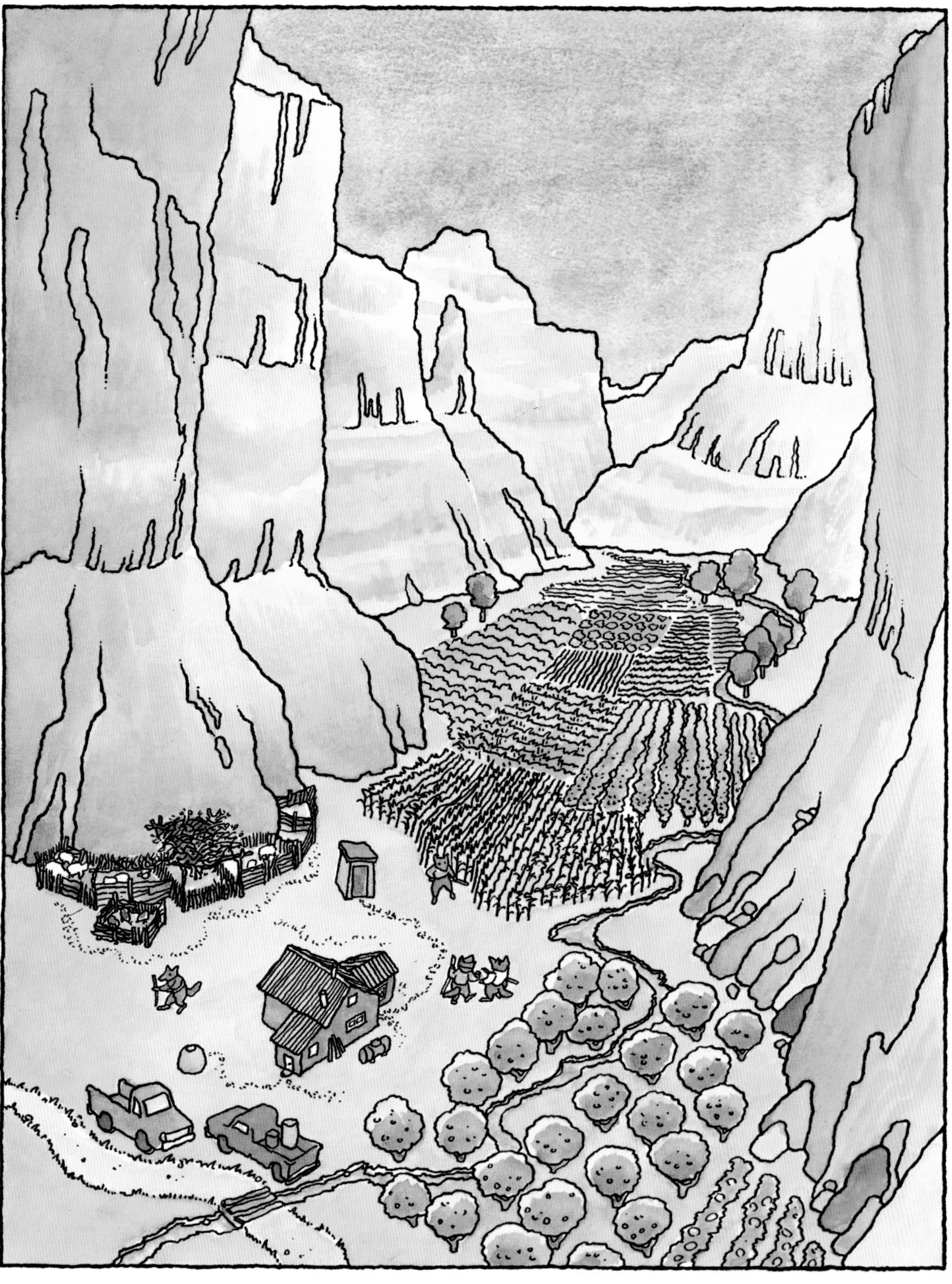

Note

The Aztec Aesop's was adapted in the 1500s by one or more Indian retellers, using a now-lost Spanish collection of the standard fables. All of these, however, can be traced to Latin and Greek manuscripts of late classical and medieval times. (For a guide, see B. E. Perry, *Babrius and Phaedrus,* Harvard, 1965.) Compared with the originals, the Aztec variants differ mainly in the cast of characters, which includes Coyote and Puma, two of the best-known animal tricksters in Native American folklore. In addition, native figures of speech have been introduced ("it settled his heart," "those words come back to bite him," "his mind was nowhere"), and a few of the stories follow a somewhat unfamiliar plot. For example, the standard tale of the fox bemused by an actor's mask that cannot speak (Perry, p. 201) becomes a fable of Coyote and a speechless statue. Entitled *Nican ompehua y çaçanillatolli...*(Here begin fable-stories...), the Aztec collection is preserved in the manuscript known as 1628-bis in the National Library of Mexico. This English retelling of twenty of the manuscript's forty-seven fables gives Coyote a larger role than he has in 1628-bis and shortens many of the morals. The collection as a whole has yet to be published in a modern language.

Annie Pennycook Elementary
3620 Fernwood Drive
Vallejo, CA 94591
(707) 556-8590